The Great
Pizza Race
and other tales of adventure

by

Jeffrey Klayman

Watermill Press

Printed in the United States of America

Illustrations by Thomas Heggie

ISBN 0-89375-828-0

Contents

Way to Go, Suzy

"Suzy, are you coming down?" shouted Mrs. Morris. "You're going to miss your bus. You don't want that to happen again."

"I'm coming, Mom," yelled Suzy. "Don't worry. I'll make it today."

"Well, you had better make it. If you're late one more time, you're in big trouble. I got a letter from your teacher yesterday. He wants to see me if you keep this up. You know I can't afford to take time off from work. So move it, now!"

"O.K., Mom, I hear you," said Suzy. She looked at herself in the mirror and hated what she saw. She was fat. "Fat Suzy"—that's what some of the kids called her. "Butterball Suzy." It made her want to cry.

She knew she had to hurry. She'd been late six times already, and the school year had just begun. But still she fussed with her hair and changed her sweater. Then she put on a different pair of jeans, but it was hopeless. Nothing looked good on her.

"What's the use?" she said aloud. "I still look like a marshmallow."

She knew that's why she was always

late. She really liked school and did well in most of her subjects. But she kept trying to put off the moment when she had to face everyone there.

"Did you finish your book report last night?" asked Mrs. Morris. "It's one thing to be late," she said. "But I want you to keep getting good grades."

"Yes, Mom," Suzy answered, looking up at the clock on the kitchen wall. "I don't have time for breakfast," she said. "I'll grab a cookie and eat it on the bus."

"Now, honey," her mother said, "that's no way to start off the day. You're still a growing girl."

"Yeah," said Suzy. "Growing the wrong way."

Mrs. Morris hugged Suzy and gave her a kiss. "Remember, you're my daughter and I love you, no matter what. O.K.?"

"O.K.," said Suzy. "And thanks, Mom.

I'll see you tonight."

Suzy grabbed her books and her jacket. She could see the bus turning up the street as she went outside. Then she stopped short and came back in.

"Now what's wrong?" asked her mother.

"My book report," said Suzy. "I left it upstairs. I have to get it."

She dashed upstairs and found the report lying on her desk. She ran down again and rushed out the door.

But it was too late. The bus was on the corner, and the doors had just closed.

"Hey wait!" cried Suzy, but the bus pulled away. "Oh, no," she said to herself. "Not again."

She was ready to give up. *What's wrong with me?* she thought. She was on the verge of tears, when suddenly she looked down and realized that she was

*"Hey wait!" cried Suzy, but the
bus pulled away.*

wearing her running shoes.

Suzy took a long, slow breath. "Well," she said. "It's now or never, so here I go!"

She started off, slowly at first, then a little faster. Suzy could still see the bus ahead, and she knew that the next stop was only three blocks away.

Her heart was pounding, but she felt excited. She used to run fast when she was a little girl. *Why not now?* she thought.

The bus turned up Harrison Avenue. Only two more blocks to go. Her hair fell down over her eyes, and her blouse was hanging out of her jacket. But something else was more important to her now.

Down Walnut Lane and up Fruitwood Road she ran until the bus stopped, and she made it. Suzy barely had the energy to climb aboard.

"Hey, Suzy," said the bus driver, "I thought we wouldn't be seeing you today."

Suzy couldn't even speak. She was out of breath, and her legs felt like rubber. The bus pulled away with a jerk and Suzy fell back. Her books flew all over.

Larry Jones jumped up out of his seat and ran over to her. "Here," he said. "Let me help you, Suzy."

Suzy looked up at him as she pulled herself together. She could hardly say, "Thanks." Larry helped her to the seat next to him and gathered her books.

"Take it easy," Larry said. "You know, that was some pretty good running you just did."

Suzy stared at him, catching her breath. "You mean you saw me chasing after the bus?" she asked.

"I sure did," answered Larry.

11

"Then why didn't you tell the bus driver?" Suzy asked. "He would have stopped."

"Well, I was going to," said Larry, "but you were really good. So I was sort of testing you."

"What do you mean?" asked Suzy.

"Do you know that you're a natural runner?" asked Larry. "You have good form, and you run with a long stride."

Suzy's breathing was becoming more normal. *Larry should know what he's talking about*, she thought. Larry was the school track star. He ran the fastest mile in the school district last spring. He was also the most handsome boy Suzy had ever seen.

"You know what?" said Larry. "I'm taking you to meet Coach Reynolds after school today. He's starting a girls' track team. I've been scouting around for some talent, and the coach has to know about you."

"I don't know," said Suzy. "In case you haven't noticed, I'm not very slender."

"Big deal," said Larry. "I was pretty chubby myself before I took up track. You'll burn off the extra weight quickly. The coach will put you on a good diet — no junk food or sugary snacks."

The bus arrived at school. Suzy's heart was pounding again. But now it was because she was happy. Larry's idea sounded good to her.

"Be at the track at three-thirty," shouted Larry as Suzy ran to her first class.

The day went fast for Suzy. After school, she hurried to the locker room to change. Outside she saw Larry talking to Coach Reynolds. About a dozen other girls were warming up on the track.

"Here she comes now," said Larry to the coach when he saw Suzy. "I'm telling you, she's good. She can really move."

"Well, we'll soon see," said the coach.

Suzy could see him looking at her. *I bet I know what he's thinking*, she said to herself. *How can that butterball move fast?* She forced a smile and walked up to him.

"O.K., Suzy," said Coach Reynolds. "Let's see what you and the other girls can do." He was not smiling, but Larry winked at her. She winked back.

The girls took their places on the starting line. They had to run one lap. That was a quarter mile. The coach blew his whistle and they were off.

It was over very fast. Suzy was not the first to finish, but she wasn't the last either.

"Not bad. Not bad at all," said the

coach to Suzy. "Larry was right. There's a runner hiding in there somewhere. Are you willing to work?" he asked.

Suzy nodded. She was still out of breath from the race. Larry gave her the O.K. sign with his hand.

The next two months were a blur to Suzy. Soon she was running all the way to school, not because she was late, but because that's what she wanted to do! She stuck to the coach's diet. After school, she did some more running, and then stretching and leg exercises.

Then came the Saturday of her first real race. Suzy was wearing a bright red warm-up suit as she jogged in place in the kitchen.

"Just one egg and a slice of toast, Mom," said Suzy, "and easy on the butter."

Mrs. Morris laughed. "Suzy," she said,

Larry gave her the O.K. sign with his hand.

"you are really amazing. This running has changed you into a new girl."

Larry was waiting at the track. He was more nervous than Suzy. He helped her stretch and jogged a little with her to help her get ready.

"Just keep relaxed," he told her. "That's important. Save yourself for the end of the race, O.K.?"

"O.K.," said Suzy, and she laughed. She had never felt better in her life.

Suzy shook her arms and legs. She got into position at the starting block. The coach raised the starting pistol and fired. *GO!*

The race was a half-mile long, and Suzy liked that distance. She paced herself and ran behind three other girls. On the last lap she burst forward.

"Way to go, Suzy! Way to go!" she heard a voice shout out from the crowd.

It was Larry. That was just what she needed to hear.

With a few more yards left, Suzy gave it her all. She moved past the girl in front and broke the tape. She collapsed on the ground, but she had won!

Coach Reynolds rushed up to her. "I'm proud of you, Suzy," he said with a smile.

Mrs. Morris and Larry came onto the track. Her mother hugged Suzy and Larry gave her a kiss. This was too much in one day. Suzy felt like laughing and crying at the same time.

"Hurry up and change," said Larry. "I'm taking you out for lunch."

"But no dessert," said Coach Reynolds. Then he added, "Well, maybe just this once. You're still in training, but you deserve it."

Suzy wasn't thinking about food as

*Suzy moved past the girl in front and
broke the tape.*

she put on her clothes. She had won a race, and now she had a date with Larry. She pulled in the belt on her jeans an extra notch. Her clothes were really getting big on her.

She stood in front of the mirror to look at herself, and this time she smiled. She liked what she saw.

"Way to go, Suzy," she said out loud. "Way to go!"

The Big Jump

It was a scorcher of a day in early July. Dogs yawned on doorsteps. Even the flies were too hot to move.

Peter Lane hurried through the heat towards the Cape Fear River. He was thinking about how good it would feel to swim in the cool water.

Matt Stuart and Jeff Reed were waiting for Peter at the old bridge. Beneath the bridge, the Cape Fear moved gently out to sea.

Matt poked Jeff when Peter came on the bridge. "Do you think he'll jump today?" Matt asked with a grin.

"Probably not," Jeff said. "It'll be just like all the other times. He's the only chicken in the Trail Club."

"Take that back," Peter said, moving towards Jeff. But Matt stopped him.

"Hey, take it easy, guys! Let's just get going, all right?"

Matt began the steep climb to the top of the bridge. Jeff followed next, and then it was Peter's turn.

It was tough going but they were used to it. Members of the Trail Club had climbed to the top many, many times.

Peter tried not to look down. He hated

to be in high places and, as usual, he wished he'd remained on the ground.

"It's too hot to stay up here," Matt said. "I say it's about time to cool off."

"I'm ready," Jeff quickly agreed.

Matt moved closer to the edge, gazed at the water below, and then leaped.

"Geronimo!"

Matt sailed through the air, and moments later, hit the water.

Jeff gave Peter a hard glance just before he jumped. "I bet you don't," Jeff said just as he, too, leaped into the Cape Fear below.

Peter stood on the edge. The water was far below, and the height made him feel strange. He bent his knees to jump but stopped. *This is crazy*, he thought.

His hands trembled as he inched away from the edge. In the distance he heard Jeff call, "I told you he'd chicken out."

*Matt moved closer to the edge, gazed at the
water below, and then leaped.*

Then there was loud laughter.

Peter tried not to listen as he climbed down. He hurried home so he would not have to face his friends.

"Did you have a good swim?" his father asked.

"Terrific," Peter muttered as he went to his room. He turned on the fan and tried to cool off.

He stared at the blades of the fan for a long, long time. Over and over again, he heard Matt and Jeff's laughter echoing in his mind. Finally, he fell asleep.

The next afternoon Peter went to a Trail Club meeting. Each summer, the club went on a trip. This year, they were going camping in the mountains near the town of Boone.

"We'll be leaving Friday," said Mr. Sloan, the leader. "That will give you enough time to check your equipment."

Peter got up to leave after the meeting, but Jeff stopped him.

"Aren't you afraid to go to the mountains?" Jeff sneered. "I mean it's wild up there. Who knows what we might find?"

"I'll be all right," Peter said gruffly.

"Just don't look down," Jeff laughed. "Hey, guys, you should have seen Peter on the bridge yesterday."

Jeff told the whole story, and the Trail Club rocked with laughter. After a while, Peter left to walk home.

"See you Friday," Mr. Sloan said.

"I'll be there," Peter answered.

By Friday morning, Peter felt better. He had packed all his gear, and he was ready for the long ride to the mountains.

The Trail Club arrived in Boone late that evening. They found a campground close to town. Early Saturday morning, Peter and the rest of the Trail Club hiked into the Blue Ridge Mountains.

Matt and Jeff were near Peter in line. But the climb was so steep that no one spoke. Peter was happy about that. He was sick of all the kidding. Besides, he was beginning to think he really was chicken.

The Trail Club hiked higher into the mountains. Below them, they could see rich valleys and hills. At dusk, they made camp.

"Remember one thing," Mr. Sloan said. "It's been dry up here so be careful with the campfire."

That night, Mr. Sloan told a ghost story about the devil's tramping ground. Even Matt and Jeff were wide-eyed and jumpy.

The next morning, a small girl's voice woke up the camp.

"I want some cereal!" she cried. Her

parents tried to calm her down. But she wandered through the campground looking for her breakfast.

"You're welcome to join us," Mr. Sloan told the strangers. Just like the Trail Club, the Wrights had come to hike and camp in the mountains. They'd been in the woods for a few days now and were low on supplies.

"We're going to hike towards Chimney Rock and then head home," Mr. Wright said. "Thanks for giving Sue the corn flakes."

The Wrights hiked up the trail while Peter and the others broke camp. Little Sue waved from the top of the closest hill. Then the Wrights disappeared into the woods.

That evening, the Trail Club camped near Bald Mountain. They were just finishing breakfast the next morning

*Little Sue waved from the top
of the closest hill.*

when Mr. and Mrs. Wright ran into their camp.

"We've lost Sue!" Mr. Wright cried. He was frantic and so was his wife. When they woke up that morning, Sue was not in their camp. They yelled and yelled, but they couldn't find her anywhere.

"We'll find her," Mr. Sloan said. "We'll break up into groups of two to begin the search."

Mr. Sloan paired Peter and Jeff together. At first Peter wanted to get a new partner. But then he realized that he would sound cowardly if he asked for one.

Jeff led the way over an old wooden bridge that crossed the river just past Hidden Falls. A deep gorge swirled below them. Once across, they hiked back towards the falls and looked for signs of the lost child.

"I don't think she'd go this far," Jeff said. "This is a long way from their camp."

"She might," Peter said.

"What do *you* know?" Jeff sneered.

"I know that we've got to keep looking," Peter replied. "I didn't ask to be your partner, so let's just make the best of it."

Jeff moved ahead in silence. "Do you smell something?" he suddenly asked. The wind swirled above them from a different direction.

"Yes, I think I do," Peter said.

There was a large group of rocks just past the falls. Beneath the rocks there was a large pool of water.

Jeff and Peter climbed to the highest point. Up ahead they saw smoke and flames.

Jeff and Peter climbed to the highest point.

"It's a forest fire!" Jeff said. "Look at it build."

The flames rose higher and higher, and because the weather was so dry, the woods burned like kindling. The gusts of wind spread the flames quickly.

"We've got to get out of here," Peter said.

"I'm for that," Jeff agreed as they ran back towards the wooden bridge. A huge spiral of smoke came from that direction, and then there was a loud crash.

"The bridge just went," Jeff said. "The whole side of this ridge is going up. We had better turn around."

They went back to the rocks and helplessly watched the flames rage out of control. The wind pushed the fire closer and closer to them while sparks twirled in the air.

"We're going to have to jump for it,"

Jeff said. He saw the fear spread across Peter's face. "You've got to this time."

Jeff went to the edge of the rocks. He was about to jump into the pool, but Peter stopped him.

"Wait a second. I thought I heard something."

"Come on," Jeff said. He leaped off the rocks and landed in the water with a splash. Then he swam to the other side of the gorge.

Peter stared at the water below. This jump was even higher than the one from the bridge at home. Then he heard a faint crying sound.

Peter turned and saw Sue crawling out from behind a rock. She was frightened and her clothes were dirty. Peter ran towards her and picked her up.

"Don't be frightened, Sue. We're going for a swim," he said. "This will be a first for both of us."

Peter held Sue tightly in his arms and went to the edge of the rock. He took a deep breath and jumped.

"Geronimooooooo!"

Peter and Sue hit the water, went under, and then surfaced. Jeff swam out to help them ashore.

"That was really something," Jeff said. On the other side of the gorge, planes dropped a group of smoke-jumpers, and they began fighting the fire.

"Let's get Sue back to her folks," Jeff said to Peter. "This is one story I've just got to tell."

Cobra

Louis Wood waited outside the principal's office. He had fallen asleep in class again. This time his teacher told him to see the principal, Mr. Carter.

Louis was called and went in. "I'm sorry, sir," he said. "I just get so bored that I doze off. I don't see the point of school. Nothing interests me."

Mr. Carter looked over Louis's records for several minutes before speaking.

"Louis," he said, "you're a bright young man. All your test scores show that you can do good work. I think what you need is a challenge. How would you like to go to work?"

Louis was shocked. "Are you kicking me out of school?"

Mr. Carter laughed. "Not at all," he explained. "We have a new work-study program. It lets students like you take a few months off to work. We hope this will give them a chance to find out what talents they have."

"What kind of job could I get?" asked Louis.

"I understand you like animals," said Mr. Carter.

"I love animals," said Louis. "I have

37

two dogs, three cats, a couple of turtles, and four baby hamsters. My home is like a zoo."

"How would you like to work in a real zoo?" asked Mr. Carter. "The Wild Animal Park needs someone. Are you interested?"

"I sure am," said Louis. He was excited now. He thanked Mr. Carter and left the office.

The next day, Louis reported to the zookeeper, Mr. Simon.

"Many school groups come to tour the zoo," Mr. Simon said. "We need someone to take them around. They will have lots of questions for you. Since you are an animal lover, it should be easy for you. How does that sound?"

"That sounds good to me," said Louis. "I've never talked to groups before, but I'm willing to try."

Louis reported to the zookeeper, Mr. Simon.

Louis liked his job. He was learning a lot about all kinds of animals. But best of all, he felt good about himself for the first time in his life. The school children looked up to him.

Louis's favorite place in the zoo was the reptile house. One day, he met a young woman there named Dr. Claire Stone.

Dr. Stone was on a special research project at the zoo. "My job is to milk the cobra snakes," she told Louis.

"Do cobras have milk?" Louis asked.

"Not exactly," said Dr. Stone. "Milking them means collecting the dangerous venom from them. The same venom that kills people can also be used to make medicines. This can save lives."

"How did you get a job like this?" asked Louis.

"I studied animal medicine. Then I

became a veterinarian," she said. "I've always had a special interest in snakes. I started working with cobras a few years ago."

Dr. Stone had a special lab in the reptile house. Louis could watch her and hear her speak through a glass window.

She opened one of the cages to show Louis a cobra. The cobra became excited and it reared up. Its neck became big and flat.

"This is called spreading its hood," Dr. Stone said. "Cobras are most dangerous at this point. This is what they do when they're ready to strike."

Louis saw that the hood had markings on it. It almost looked like a human face. It was very pretty.

Dr. Stone used a pole with a forked tip to hold the snake. At the right moment she quickly grabbed the cobra at the

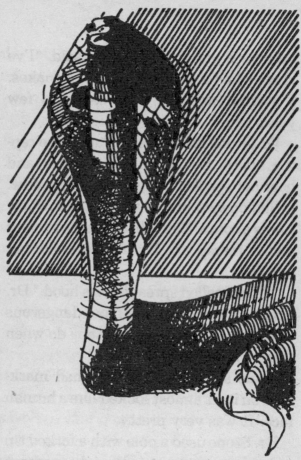

The cobra became excited and it reared up.

back of its neck. Then she put the snake's mouth on a special bottle that was covered with a thin sheet of rubber. The cobra sank its sharp fangs into the sheet. Louis could see drops of the deadly venom trickling into the bottle.

"Some cobra venom can be very helpful to people," she said. "We're only just starting to find all the uses for it."

Louis decided to go back to school when the work-study program was over. *I want to work with animals the way Dr. Stone does. I want to help people, too,* he thought.

On his last day at the zoo, Louis took a group of children through the reptile house. Dr. Stone was getting ready to milk a big cobra that had just arrived at the zoo.

Louis told the children about Dr. Stone's work. Suddenly, some of the

43

kids pointed to the lab in horror. One girl started to scream.

Louis whirled around and looked through the window. What he saw made him gasp. Dr. Stone was in one corner of the lab. A few feet from her was the big cobra. Its hood was spread and Louis could see that it was ready to strike. Dr. Stone could not reach the snake pole. It was too far away.

Without thinking, Louis ran around to the back of the lab. The door was not locked and he came in slowly.

"Louis, get out of here," said Dr. Stone. "Call the zookeeper. He'll know what to do."

"There's no time," Louis said. "I can't leave you like this."

Louis saw the pole lying a few feet behind the cobra. He walked over to it and bent down to pick it up.

A few feet from Dr. Stone was the big cobra.

Suddenly, the cobra turned away from Dr. Stone and came towards Louis. He grabbed the pole just in time. The cobra tried to strike. But Louis pushed it away with the pole.

"I'm going to try for the cobra," said Dr. Stone. She slowly moved behind the snake. Then, in one quick movement, she grabbed the snake at the back of its neck. The snake's mouth opened wide and venom dripped from its fangs.

Quickly she dropped the snake into its cage and slammed it shut.

Louis dropped the pole. For the first time he was aware of how scared he had been. His whole body was trembling. He could feel his heart pounding with fear.

"It all happened so quickly," said Dr. Stone. "I forgot to lock the cage when I went to get the milking bottle. The cobra crawled out onto the floor. You can never be too careful with snakes."

"I'm glad I was here," said Louis, forcing a smile. When he left the lab, his legs felt weak. He could barely walk.

The school children clapped when Louis returned.

"That was great," one boy said. "I'm coming back tomorrow. Can you do that again for us?"

Louis laughed. "Come back in about ten years," he said. "I'll be here. Only then, I'll be Dr. Louis Wood."

The Great
Pizza Race

Willy read the sign in the window of Ben's
Pizza Shop—DELIVERY PERSON
NEEDED. It seemed like the answer to
all Willy's problems. He went in to apply
for the job.

"I need someone who's really fast,"
said Ben. "People want their pizzas hot."

"Oh, I'm fast," said Willy. "You'll be

very happy with me."

"I was really hoping for someone with a car," said Ben, "but I'll try you out for a few days."

"Thanks," said Willy. "My dad's been sick and couldn't work for a while. Now I can help out."

Willy started the next day. He wore his sneakers. As soon as the first pie came out of the oven, Ben put it in a box. Willy grabbed it and ran out of the store.

"Wait!" Ben shouted. "You don't know where it's going."

"Yes I do," said Willy. "I heard you take the order on the phone." He ran the three blocks to an office building. The elevator was full, so Willy ran up five flights of stairs to the office.

"There you are, sir, nice and hot," said Willy as he handed the pie to the man.

Willy ran up five flights of stairs to the office.

Willy ran back to the store and made five more deliveries over the next few hours. By the end of the day, he was tired but happy.

The next day, Ben looked upset when Willy came in. He told Willy he had some bad news for him.

"A guy named Al stopped by last night," Ben said. "He was looking for work."

"But you don't need anyone else," said Willy. "You have me."

"Al has a car," Ben explained. "He can deliver all over town."

"I'll be faster," said Willy. "I promise I will."

"You're going as fast as anyone on two feet can go," said Ben. "I'm really sorry. I have to think about business."

"I understand," said Willy. He needed the job, but he knew that Ben had to do what was best for business.

There were still orders to go out that day. Ben put two pizzas on the counter, and Willy took off with them. As he ran, he thought about how much his job meant to him.

Then, as he was rounding a corner, a girl on a skateboard almost ran right into him. "I'm really sorry," the girl said. "I forget how fast these things can go. I was late for my dance class, and I just wasn't looking."

Willy watched the girl go off. She was able to pass all the cars that were stuck in the heavy traffic.

The idea came to him in a flash. *That's it!* thought Willy. *With a skateboard, I can get all over town, too.*

He delivered the pizzas and ran back to tell Ben his idea.

Ben thought about it for a moment. "I

don't know," he said. "A car can still go much faster than a skateboard."

"Not always," said Willy. "When there's lots of traffic, a skateboard is faster. I can jump on the sidewalk if I have to, and I don't have to find a place to park."

"I feel awful about this," said Ben. "I already told Al he could start tomorrow."

"Give me a chance on the skateboard," said Willy. "If I'm not faster than him, he can have the job."

"Well, it sounds a bit crazy, but O.K.," said Ben.

After work, Willy got out his old pair of roller skates. He took the wheels off the skates. Then he found a good, strong piece of wood for his skateboard.

Willy worked hard, and a few hours later, he had his skateboard. *It's not like a store-bought one*, he thought. *But I don't care, as long as it's fast.*

He left for work early the next day. On the way, he practiced on his skateboard.

When Willy got to the shop, he met Al. Al told Willy that he needed the job to save money for college.

"I wish I could hire both of you," said Ben, "but I just can't afford to right now."

Before long, the phone started ringing, and Ben took orders for six pies. Soon the pies were ready.

Ben told Willy and Al that he would give them each three pies. The one who could deliver the pies and get back to the store first would keep the job.

Al and Willy picked up their pies and started out.

Willy raced downtown on his skateboard. He made it in less than ten

Willy raced downtown on his skateboard.

minutes. He tried not to think about how Al was doing.

He had dropped off two pies and was on his way to drop off the third when it happened. Somehow, as he was trying to jump a curb, his skateboard went flying out from under him, and he fell. The pizza pie flew out of his hands and landed upside down in the street. A big truck ran over it.

Willy picked himself up. He had skinned both his knees, but he was too upset to notice.

Well, that's that! Willy thought. The pizza was spread all over the pavement in a big red and yellow mess.

Willy was ready to give up and go home. Then he thought about the people waiting for their pizza.

Willy raced back to the store, and Ben gave him a fresh pizza. Willy jumped back on his skateboard and delivered it.

He returned to say good-bye to Ben when he was through. "Thanks for giving me a chance," Willy said. "I did the best I could. I can't compete with a car."

Ben smiled. "Young man, it looks as if you've got yourself a job," he said.

"How can that be?" Willy asked. "Al must have gotten back before me."

"Al just called," Ben explained. "He had a flat tire on the way back. He's fixing it now at a gas station."

"Wow, then I won!" Willy exclaimed. He was happy, but he felt badly that Al would not have a job.

Willy went to deliver some more pies. When he got back, Al was there.

"I'm sorry you lost, Al," said Willy. "You needed the job as much as I did."

"Oh, but I have good news about that," said Al. "While I was fixing my flat, the owner of the station offered me a job pumping gas and changing tires. It looks as if we both won."

"That's great," said Willy. "Things couldn't have worked out better for both of us."

Ben took a large pie out of the oven. "Where's this one going to?" asked Willy, as he grabbed it off the counter.

"This one's staying right here," said Ben. "It's for you and Al. You both deserve it."

"I Hear You, Loud and Clear!"

The small plane touched down gently at Westbriar Airport. Tom Connors waved the big torch lights and guided the plane to the gate.

"Last one tonight?" asked George, as Tom came in and sat on a stool in the airport coffee shop.

"That's it, George," said Tom. "How's the apple pie tonight?"

"Tom, I've been meaning to ask you something," said George. "I don't understand why you're still on the ground crew. I thought you passed your exam for air-traffic controller years ago."

Tom avoided looking at George as he spoke. "You must have noticed by now that I stutter badly sometimes," he said.

"So what?" asked George. "You must have noticed by now that I'm growing bald." George laughed his big laugh. Tom had to smile in spite of himself.

"It's different," said Tom. "I speak well most of the time, but under pressure I can't get a word out. The board wouldn't pass me. I can't really blame them."

"But this airport is so small," said

"How's the apple pie tonight?"

George. "No more than a half-dozen planes take off or land here in a day."

"It doesn't matter," said Tom. "I really thought I could overcome my speech problem and get the job. But on the interview, I just fell apart. I guess I'm stuck on the ground."

Tom paid for his pie and coffee and decided to go up to the control tower. Now that it was dark, his friend Shawn would be closing up for the night.

"Hey, Tom, how's it going?" asked Shawn. "There's a big storm coming up. I just heard it over the radio."

"Do you mind if I stick around a while?" asked Tom. "I like to keep in shape on the radar controls."

"It's all yours, my friend," said Shawn. "I want to get home before this storm hits."

Tom loved being in the control tower

by himself. He stayed late every chance he got. He sat down in the big chair and looked out at the deserted airport.

He switched on the controls and pulled the headset on over his ears. He stared at the round screen as the radar scanned the sky for aircraft.

Tom stared at the radio microphone on the desk in front of him. He pulled it close and started speaking.

"This is Westbriar," he said. "You're cleared for landing on Runway Number One. Do you read me? Over and out."

Tom spoke perfectly. He did not stutter once.

Why can I do it now when there's no one listening? he wondered. *Having an audience should not make me stutter.*

Suddenly, there was a blinding flash of lightning and loud claps of thunder. Then the landing lights on the runway went dark. The storm had knocked out all the power.

I guess I'll be going home, thought Tom as he looked at the controls. The radar screen was still working. The control tower had its own power supply for situations like this one.

He took off the headset and started to leave. But then he heard a crackling sound coming from the headset and saw a blip on the radar screen. A small plane was in the area.

Tom put the headset back on. He could hear a voice now coming through the static.

"Piper 420 calling Westbriar. Do you read me? Please come in. Over and out."

Tom's heart seemed to skip a beat. He picked up the microphone, and his hand shook so badly that he almost dropped it.

The voice came on again. "Come in, somebody, please. Request instructions for emergency landing. Over and out."

Tom felt his throat tighten, and he could barely swallow. No words would come from his lips. It was as if someone had stolen his tongue.

"We're lost and almost out of fuel," came the voice over the radio. "We're being tossed around like a feather up here. Please come in."

Tom cleared his throat and spoke. "H-hello, Piper. Th-this is Westbriar." His speech was shaky, but the words were coming out.

"Request flight pattern for landing. I can't climb because my dials are all broken, and I can't see anything."

"Our lights are out," Tom said in a clearer voice. "The wind is so strong now, I can't even light a flare."

65

"Can you talk us down?" came the voice from the Piper.

Tom fought the panic that was rising up inside of him. "Hang on, Piper," he answered. He saw the plane clearly now on the radar screen.

"You're ten miles away," Tom said. "Hang on. Over." He ran to the phone and dialed Shawn's number. There was no answer. Tom realized it was up to him as he ran back to the controls.

"How much fuel do you have left?" asked Tom.

"Not much," answered the Piper. "There's just about fifteen minutes' worth."

Tom's back was covered with sweat. He did not even stop to realize how well he had been speaking. "Your instructions are to keep on a southerly course," he said. "We'll get you down."

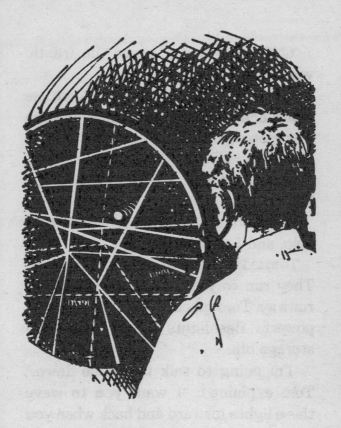

*Tom saw the plane clearly now on
the radar screen.*

"O.K., but hurry," came the frantic voice over the radio.

Tom had an idea. He dashed down the stairs and into the coffee shop. George was groping his way around in the dark.

"You're still here?" asked George. "I can't see a thing. I was sure you had left."

"Listen to me," said Tom. "I need your help, and I need it now."

Tom led George outside into the storm. They ran to the supply shed near the runway. Tom quickly pulled down some powerful flashlights that were kept in a storage bin.

"I'm going to talk the plane down," Tom explained. "I want you to wave these lights forward and back when you hear the plane overhead. It's our only chance of bringing in the plane."

Tom dashed back to the control tower

and spoke into the microphone. "I can see you on the radar. You're right on course. Tell me if you can see the waving lights," he said.

"I can see them," came the excited voice of the pilot.

"Our runway is only 4000 feet," said Tom. "Is that clear? Please respond. Over."

"I read you," said the pilot. "I've never landed on such a small strip before, but I have no choice now."

"Start dropping now," said Tom. His voice was strong and steady. He could hear the plane's engine growing very loud. Then, he saw the plane's lights. It was heading straight for the control tower. It was going to crash.

"Climb, climb!" Tom shouted over the radio. "Circle and try again. Approach more from the west to allow for the strong wind."

The plane barely cleared the tower. Tom could see George waving his arms on the runway strip.

The next approach was better. Tom could see the plane's lights a few hundred yards off.

"O.K.," said Tom. "You're looking good to me—right on course. Drop your nose a little more. "

The engine strained against the strong winds.

"Keep steady," said Tom. "You're almost here. Just a little more and— NOW, SET HER DOWN!"

The plane's wheels touched down and bounced on the tarred surface of the runway. It veered off and came to a screeching halt a few feet from the window of George's coffee shop.

Tom was drenched with sweat. He

*The plane came to a screeching halt a few feet
from the window of George's coffee shop.*

jumped up and ran down to the plane. He helped the pilot to the ground and into the coffee shop. George ran up and joined them. George gave the "thumbs-up" signal to Tom.

"I owe you my life," the pilot told Tom.

"I was worried you wouldn't understand a word I said," Tom replied.

"Oh, I heard you," said the pilot. "Every single word—loud and clear!"

Whiteout!

Dan Simpson looked out the window of the plane and saw nothing but white. Ice and snow were everywhere. Then, as the plane started to land, he could make out a few small huts and a group of people.

Dan's Uncle Joe met him as he stepped off the plane. "Welcome to the South Pole," he said.

This visit was a big thrill for Dan. He hadn't seen his uncle in almost a year. Uncle Joe had come to the South Pole to study the weather.

It was late evening, but the sky was still bright. "It's so strange to see the sun out at this time," Dan said. "How do you know when to go to sleep?"

"During the summer, we have sunlight twenty-four hours a day," Uncle Joe explained. "All of us work very hard here at the ice station. No one has trouble falling asleep."

Dan looked forward to the month ahead. The South Pole was so beautiful. He took pictures of everything he saw.

"It's like being on a strange planet," he said. "When I get home, I'm going to give a talk to my science class and show slides."

They reached the base camp of the ice

station. There were four long huts that were used for sleeping and eating. There were also a half dozen bigger huts where Dan's uncle and the others did their work.

Inside the hut, they were greeted by Bravo, a big gray-and-white husky. "Bravo will be your dog during your visit," said Dan's uncle. "He was raised here and knows his way around. He can even find his way during a whiteout."

"What's a whiteout?" asked Dan.

"It's a thick fog that falls when the clouds are very low. In a whiteout, you can't even see what's right in front of you. People can get lost and freeze to death, even though they're just a few feet from safety."

"That sounds scary," said Dan.

"It can be," said Uncle Joe. "Don't go anywhere by yourself, even if it's just outside the hut."

Dan and his uncle were greeted by Bravo,
a big gray-and-white husky.

"Oh, I promise," said Dan.

Dan went to sleep with Bravo lying at the foot of his bed. Outside, he heard the wind blowing. *Home seems a million miles away*, he thought. He pulled the blanket up around his ears.

The first week went quickly for Dan. He got up early every morning and helped his uncle take readings of the weather.

"We can learn a lot from these readings," said Uncle Joe. "Much of the weather around the world begins here. That's why it's important to study it."

One day, Dan helped his uncle pull up buckets of water from a big hole in the ice. "We're looking for forms of life that can live in this icy water," Uncle Joe said.

On the way back to the ice station, they passed a herd of seals. The seals were lying on a large chunk of ice. "There must be hundreds of them," said Dan. "Why didn't I bring my camera with me?"

As their truck got closer to the seals, one of them threw back its head. Then it made a strange barking noise.

"It sounds as if he's saying hello to us," said Dan.

"Not really," said Uncle Joe. "That's a bull seal. He's telling us to stay away. This is his land and he doesn't want strangers coming to visit. Seals can get pretty mean when they're angry."

Soon, Dan's month at the Ice Station was almost up. One Sunday morning, everyone got up extra early. A ship was coming with food, mail, and supplies. Because of the ice, the ship only came a few times a year.

Dan and Bravo rode in a jeep with

Uncle Joe. When they reached the ship, Uncle Joe got out to help load the supplies onto trucks. Bravo ran off to play with the other dogs.

"This time, I brought my camera and lots of film," said Dan. "I want to get pictures of everything."

"O.K.," said Uncle Joe, "but stay close by. Remember what I told you."

"Don't worry," said Dan. "I'll be careful."

Dan took some shots of the crew unloading huge crates from the ship. Then he walked back to the jeep for some more film. He heard the sound of seals barking. He turned around and saw dozens of baby seals on an ice floe not far from the ship.

That's great, Dan thought. *I can get some great shots of them.*

He walked a few feet to the baby

seals. They seemed to be playing tag. They chased each other over the ice until one of them fell into the water.

While Dan was watching the seals, he lost track of the time. Before he knew it, he had used up all his film. He turned to go back to the jeep. He walked a few feet but couldn't see anything. He turned around to where the baby seals were, but he could no longer see them.

Oh, no, Dan thought. *It's a whiteout! I'm lost. I can't see anything.*

He heard some sounds and tried to follow them. But he wasn't sure which way to go. Suddenly, he had the feeling that he was moving. He took a step and almost fell into the water.

Dan knew that he was on a piece of ice that had broken off and was floating away.

"Help me!" he shouted. "Someone

*Before Dan knew it, he had used up
all his film.*

please help me!"

It was starting to get much colder. Dan had neither food nor water with him. He wondered how long the whiteout would last.

He thought he heard a noise. It sounded like barking. "Bravo!" he cried out. "Is that you? I'm over here, boy." He couldn't see anything, but the sound was getting closer.

Just then, he felt another piece of ice break off under his feet. He jumped, hoping he would not land in the icy water.

He landed hard on the ice and fell on his face. He felt the frozen snow sting his nose and lips. For a moment, he couldn't breathe. Then he felt a warm tongue on his face.

"It's you, Bravo," Dan said, hugging the dog. "You found me."

Dan felt the ice start to break again. He and Bravo leaped again and landed on solid ice this time.

In a few minutes, the whiteout started to clear. Dan was surprised to see that he was very close to the ship. He ran over to where his uncle was waiting for him.

"I should be angry with you," said Uncle Joe. "You gave us all a scare, but at least you're safe."

"Thanks to Bravo here," said Dan.

"Don't ever go off like that again," said Dan's uncle.

"I won't," said Dan. "Besides, by this time next week, I'll be back home. Something tells me I won't feel like going skiing this winter. I've had enough snow for a long, long time."

Alibi Witness

Lynn Davies looked at the window display in the camera shop. She pressed her nose to the glass. There was the one she had to have. It was a thirty-five millimeter with a zoom lens, the kind press photographers use.

Lynn reached into her pocket and felt

her money. She had just withdrawn two hundred dollars from the bank. It was all the money she had. She was supposed to be saving it for college. But she just had to have that camera.

Half an hour later, Lynn walked out of the store with her camera. Her heart was pounding with excitement. She had bought film and was ready to take pictures.

"I'm going to be a photojournalist," she had told the salesperson. "Some day, you're going to see a picture in the papers. And underneath it will say *Photo by Lynn Davies*."

Lynn looked out over Main Street. Early that morning, it had snowed for the first time that season. The snow covered the streets and the tops of the buildings. She put the camera to her eye and tried it out.

"Hey, Lynn," came a familiar voice. "Take my picture. You can send it to all the magazines."

Lynn turned and saw a young man in the view finder. He was wearing a bright red jogging suit. His navy blue stocking cap was pulled down over his face to keep him warm.

"Who's that?" Lynn called out.

The jogger pulled the cap off. "It's me, Billy Henley," he answered. "Don't tell me you don't recognize your old school friend."

"It could have been anybody with that cap pulled down," said Lynn.

"It's the new me," said Billy, jogging in place. "I'm keeping in shape now and starting a whole new life."

Lynn smiled. She was happy to see Billy trying so hard. He had been in some trouble with the police several

"It's me, Billy Henley."

years ago. But during the past year, he had gotten a job and was going to night school to study computers.

Lynn focused the camera and snapped Billy's picture. He waved and ran off. Lynn snapped another half-dozen shots of Billy before he turned the corner.

That night after dinner, Lynn went down to the basement. She had built her own darkroom there. She had an enlarger and all the equipment she needed.

She mixed the chemicals to develop her prints. She turned on the special safelight. Then she unloaded the roll of film from her new camera.

Several hours later she was finished. She proudly examined her day's work.

Well, they're not going to make the front page of any newspaper, she thought. *But they're not bad.* Each picture was sharp and clear. She couldn't wait to give blowups of the pictures to Billy.

The next morning, Lynn went downstairs for breakfast. She planned to spend the day taking pictures.

Her sister greeted Lynn with a frown. "Look at the front page of the newspaper," she said. "What a shame! Everybody thought he was going to turn out all right."

"Who are you talking about?" asked Lynn. She picked up the *Times Herald* and saw the headline:

LOCAL BOY HELD
ON ROBBERY CHARGES.

Underneath was a picture of Billy Henley.

Lynn collapsed into her seat. She was stunned. "But I just saw him yesterday," she said. "I took his picture."

She read the article. It said that a young man wearing a bright red jogging suit and a stocking cap robbed Fred's Market at ten-thirty in the morning. Based on the store owner's description, the police picked up Billy Henley several hours later.

Lynn could not eat her breakfast. She kept staring at Billy's picture. "How can it be?" she said out loud. "I just know that he's innocent."

Lynn thought of the pictures she was going to give Billy. *All that is changed now*, she thought. *I'm sure Billy doesn't want to look at pictures.*

She went down to her darkroom and looked at her photos of Billy. *There must be something I can do*, she thought. All at once it came to her – the pictures, the robbery!

The newspapers said the store was robbed at ten-thirty. Lynn ran upstairs to call the police. She told the officer

Lynn could not eat her breakfast.

that she was with Billy at the time of the robbery.

Then she grabbed the photos and raced down to the police station. The sergeant on duty looked over them carefully.

"You could have taken these photos any time," he said. "It could have been yesterday, or last week, or last month."

"But there's snow on the ground," Lynn said. "We had the first snowfall yesterday. That proves it, doesn't it?"

"Maybe that proves it was yesterday," said the sergeant. "We still need to know the time."

Lynn left the station. Her mind was racing as she walked up Main Street. She stopped at the spot where she had taken Billy's picture.

Then she noticed it. She was facing the Village Book Mart. Through the front window she could see a clock on the back wall of the shop.

Lynn hurried home and ran down to her darkroom. She put each negative in the enlarger and looked at them one by one. In one picture she saw what she was hoping to find. She could see the clock through the window of the Book Mart in the picture. But she couldn't make out the time.

Lynn took out the negative. She put black tape around the part of the negative that showed the clock. This is called cropping. In this manner, she would be able to enlarge only the part of the picture she wanted.

It was hard work. Lynn had to get the store clock in focus so she could make out the time. Her eyes were so tired that she could hardly see. Finally, she had a clear print.

"I was right," she cried. "The time was

In one picture Lynn saw what she was hoping to find.

ten-thirty. That proves Billy's not the robber."

Lynn did not even wait for the print to dry. She went back to the police station and showed the photo to the sergeant.

The sergeant looked at the picture. He asked Lynn to have a seat in the waiting room.

Lynn waited for a long time. Then the door opened and Billy Henley came out. Lynn ran up to him.

"I feel dazed," said Billy. "All this has been a nightmare for me. I don't know how to thank you."

"Don't thank me," said Lynn. "Thank my camera!"

The next day, Lynn came down to breakfast. The morning newspaper was lying on the kitchen table. The headline read:

PHOTO FREES ROBBERY SUSPECT

There was Lynn's picture of Billy Henley and underneath it were the words: *Photo by Lynn Davies.*